*millennium*

To

_____

_____

From

_____

_____

_____

# The Story of
# Millennia
# the Angel

*A fable of hope for a
new generation*

*Giles Andreae*
*Michael Foreman*

PROSPERO
B·O·O·K·S
A DIVISION OF CHAPTERS INC.

*A* great celebration was planned for the World
As the century came to an end.
The kings and the queens of each country on Earth
Had been waiting for years to attend.

*Great artists and sculptors had crafted her form,*

*Every inch was titanium smooth,*

*And a billion computer chips inside her wings*

*Could precisely control how she'd move.*

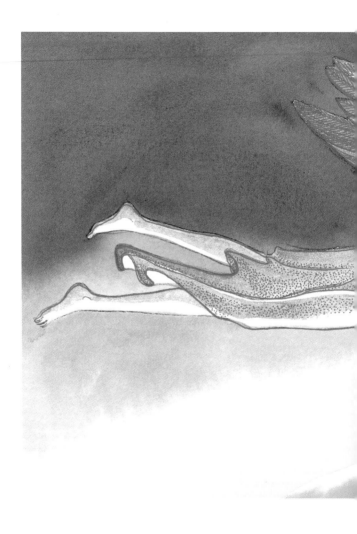

*But, as the horizon was lit by the dawn,*

*And the people looked up to the sky,*

*Millennia opened her wings to the wind*

*And discovered she just couldn't fly.*

She started to stagger and lurch through the crowd
And they watched without making a sound.
Then, all of a sudden, Millennia stumbled
And fell, with a crash, to the ground.

The monarchs and scientists looked on, amazed,

"What on earth can have happened?" they cried.

And then one little boy scurried out from the crowd

And he ran to Millennia's side.

"You've thought about every last detail," he said,

"Yet you've left out the most vital part.

How can Millennia possibly fly

When she hasn't been given a heart?"

Very gently, he clambered up onto her back
As the people stood back in surprise.
"Let me be your heart for the future," he said,
And then, slowly, she started to rise.

Millennia glided up into the sky

And the crowds below started to roar.

She felt the warm wind rolling under her wings

Like waves rolling into the shore.

And as they flew higher, the little boy laughed.

"I will always be with you," he said.

Millennia soared through the wide open sky

And she smiled at the future ahead.

*This poem was specially commissioned for the*
*Selfridges Christmas Millennium windows.*

*This edition produced in 1999*
*for Prospero Books*
*a division of Chapters Inc.*
*First published in Great Britain by Orchard Books in 1999.*
1 84121 605 4
*Text © Purple Enterprises Limited 1999*
*Illustrations © Michael Foreman 1999*
*The rights of Giles Andreae to be identified as the author and*
*Michael Foreman to be identified as the illustrator have been*
*asserted by them in accordance with the*
*Copyright, Designs and Patents Act, 1988.*
*A CIP catalogue record for this book is available from the British Library*
1 3 5 7 9 10 8 6 4 2
*Printed in Belgium*

**TALBOT** @Henry05 Do you think there's anywhere I could get a St. Crispin's Day card at this time of night?
*8:51 PM 24th Oct 1415 from LongBowMobile*

**GLOUCESTER** @Henry05 "hold their manhoods cheap" LOL.
*8:52 PM 24th Oct 1415 from Raspberry*

**TALBOT** @Henry05 I suppose I could MAKE her a St. Crispin's Day card; they say it's more personal but I think it just looks cheap.
*8:54 PM 24th Oct 1415 from LongBowMobile*

**GLOUCESTER** @Henry05 Get it? "Hold their manhoods"
*8:56 PM 24th Oct 1415 from Raspberry*

**LeDauphin** @Henry05 Venez ici pour l'essayer si vous vous croyez assez dur.
*9:04 PM 24th Oct 1415 from ArmagnacSurLigne*

# #THEGREATWALL OFCHINA

**ChienFu** @YungFa I'm telling you, I'm there right now and
it's nowhere near finished.
*2:15 PM 12th Jan 1452 from MingNet*

**YungFa** @ChienFu How nowhere near finished?
*2:16 PM 12th Jan 1452 from LiaodongOnLine*

**ChienFu** @YungFa SERIOUSLY nowhere near. Cement's not dry
on the Juyongguan stretch and they haven't even started the
Mutianyu section.
*2:18 PM 12th Jan 1452 from MingNet*

**YungFa** @ChienFu Oh FFS. What's the bloody excuse this time?
*2:19 PM 12th Jan 1452 from LiaodongOnLine*

**ChienFu** @YungFa Buggered if I know, there's nobody
even here to ask.
*2:21 PM 12th Jan 1452 from MingNet*

**ChienFu** @YungFa They FINALLY showed up about four o'clock.
*6:17 PM 12th Jan 1452 from MingNet*

**YungFa** @ChienFu What? Where had they all been?
*6:18 PM 12th Jan 1452 from LiaodongOnLine*

**ChienFu** @YungFa I did ask. Rather forcefully. "Got a Temple
roofing job on the go in Gansu province" says the foreman.
Nearly punched him.
*6:19 PM 12th Jan 1452 from MingNet*